Adventures
with
Barefoot
Critters

An ABC Book by Teagan White

TUNDRA BOOKS

Copyright © 2014 by Teagan White

Published in Canada by Tundra Books,
a division of Random House of Canada Limited,
a Penguin Random House Company

Published in the United States by Tundra Books of Northern New York,
P.O. Box 1030, Plattsburgh, New York 12901

Library of Congress Control Number: 2013940754

Library and Archives Canada Cataloguing in Publication

White, Teagan, author, illustrator
Adventures with barefoot critters / written and illustrated
by Teagan White.

Issued in print and electronic formats.
ISBN 978-1-77049-624-8 (bound).—ISBN 978-1-77049-626-2 (epub)

1. English language—Alphabet—Juvenile literature.
2. Alphabet books. 3. Animals—Pictorial works—Juvenile literature. 4.
Seasons—Pictorial works—Juvenile literature. I. Title.

PE1155.W482 2014   j421'.1   C2013-903529-X
C2013-903530-3

Edited by Samantha Swenson
The artwork in this book was rendered in watercolor and gouache.
The type in this book was set in Stanyan.
Printed and bound in Hong Kong

www.penguinrandomhouse.ca

6 7 8 9 10 21 20 19 18 17 16

TUNDRA BOOKS | Penguin
Random
House

For anyone who went out and explored
while everyone else was bored

In January we clean the **attic** and try on old clothes.

 And we **build a bridge** out of **branches** over the river that froze.

 In February we **catch colds** and **can't** go out to play.

 But when we feel better
we **dance all day**.

 We like to help Robin
keep her **eggs** warm.

And in March we **feed** ducks in a light rainstorm.

 We work hard in April
to help new plants **grow**.

 And borrow **honey** from **hives** while the bees say **hello**.

 In May we're **inventors** who **imagine** rockets to the moon.

 Then we cast off
our jackets on
warm afternoons.

By June all our kites get
knotted or break...

 So we **leave** them behind
to go jump in the **lake**!

 We **make messes** with **mud**
when it rains in July.

 But we take **nice** long **naps** in the grass once it's dry.

We collect things
the **ocean** washed up
on the shore.

P And in August we enjoy
a **picnic** for four.

We use **quilts** to build
a tall fort for the **queen**.

And in September
we **rake** leaves that
are no longer green.

 On cool days we set ships
to sail in the stream.

 And in October,
trick-or-treating's
a scream!

We make cozy campfires
and eat **under** the stars.

And in November our relatives **visit** from afar.

In cold **weather we write**
letters to good friends
who go...

To places marked **X**,
far away from the snow.

 In December our **yard** is an ice-skating rink.

We stay up just till
New Year, then fall
asleep in a wink!

zzzzzz